# Miranda

## AND

# MAUDE

1

written by
# EMMA WUNSCH

illustrated by
# JESSIKA VON INNEREBNER

Amulet Books
New York

# MIRANDA AND MAUDE ①

# THE PRINCESS AND THE
## Absolutely NOT a Princess

Library of Congress Cataloging-in-Publication Data
Names: Wunsch, Emma, author. | Von Innerebner, Jessika, illustrator.
Title: The princess and the-absolutely-not-a-princess / by Emma Wunsch ; Illustrated
by Jessika von Innerebner.
Description: New York : Amulet Books, 2018. | Series: Miranda and Maude ; volume 1
| Summary: Princess Miranda is horrified when her parents insist she attend public
school, especially because Maude, who sits next to her in 3B, is everything the princess
finds most offensive.
Identifiers: LCCN 2017052443 | ISBN 978-1-4197-3179-2 (hardcover POB)
Subjects: | CYAC: Schools—Fiction. | Princesses—Fiction. | Social
action—Fiction. | Friendship—Fiction.
Classification: LCC PZ7.1.W97 Pri 2018 | DDC [E]—dc23

Printed and bound in U.S.A.
10 9 8 7 6 5 4 3 2 1

Amulet Books are available at special discounts when
purchased in quantity for premiums and promotions as
well as fundraising or educational use. Special editions can
also be created to specification. For details, contact
specialsales@abramsbooks.com or the address below.

ABRAMS The Art of Books
195 Broadway, New York, NY 10007
abramsbooks.com

FOR ANYONE WHO HAS
EVER GONE TO SCHOOL.

# 1

# PRINCESS MIRANDA DOES NOT WANT TO GO TO SCHOOL

It was Princess Miranda's first first day of school. She had never been to school before, and she absolutely, positively did not want to go.

But she was going!

Just one hour ago, her parents, the king and queen, had woken her up and said, "Time to go to school!"

At first, Miranda had thought she was dreaming. She was a princess! She lived in an enormous castle filled with fancy and expensive things. She didn't get woken up and told to go to school. She had a wonderful, very old royal tutor named Madame Cornelia who came at noon, napped at one, and left promptly at two.

But apparently, things had changed.

Because here she was. Curled up in the back of a fancy automobile being driven to school.

Miranda's mother, whom the princess called QM (which was short for Queen Mom), squeezed her daughter's hand.

"You might like it," QM whispered, as Blake, the driver of the fancy automobile, turned into a parking lot with a sign that said MOUNTAIN RIVER VALLEY ELEMENTARY SCHOOL.

The princess shook her head. She knew she would absolutely, positively hate school.

# THE PRINCESS GETS
# OUT OF THE CAR

As soon as the royal automobile stopped, a tall man with a long, curling mustache ran over.

"HOW DO YOU DO?" the tall man boomed. "I'M PRINCIPAL FISH!" He clutched a very thick book against the middle of his chest.

"Lovely to meet you," QM said. She looked at Miranda, who was looking at her feet and wondering what would happen to her fancy shoes. Miranda had a feeling that school was full of dirt and sand and glue, all of which could ruin her beautiful shoes.

"HERE'S A COPY OF THE *OFFICIAL RULES OF MOUNTAIN RIVER VALLEY ELEMENTARY.*

IT HAS EVERY SINGLE RULE OF THE SCHOOL. IT'S VERY USEFUL," Principal Fish yelled, holding out the thick book.

"Thank you," replied QM.

"AND NOW I'LL TAKE YOU TO MEET YOUR TEACHER," hollered Principal Fish. "NORMALLY STUDENTS ARE NOT ALLOWED IN UNTIL SEVEN FORTY-TWO, BUT BECAUSE YOU'RE NEW, YOU'RE NOT BREAKING RULE NUMBER FORTY-SIX!"

If Princess Miranda noticed how loudly Principal Fish spoke, she didn't show it. Still looking down at her shoes, she followed QM and Principal Fish inside Mountain River Valley Elementary, which smelled revoltingly like hard-boiled eggs, which the princess despised. As soon as she was old enough to speak, she had forbidden hard-boiled eggs inside the castle.

The princess held her breath as Principal Fish walked them past the gymnasium (which smelled like socks), his office (which smelled like onions and old fish), and the library (which smelled like joy and cinnamon). He took a left at the cafeteria and walked down the hall, until he reached a room with a sign on the door that said 3B in bright yellow letters.

"THREE B!" Principal Fish shouted. "MIRANDA, THIS IS YOUR CLASSROOM!"

"And I'll be your teacher," a young woman with brown hair said from the doorway. "I'm Miss Kinde. That's kind with an *e*." Her voice was soothing and quiet.

Miranda looked confused.

"She's not a great speller," QM said. "She's probably behind in math and science, too. Her royal tutor . . ." QM wasn't quite sure how to explain Madame Cornelia to Miss Kinde, so she looked at her daughter, who wasn't listening to her, because she was still looking down.

*Shoes this nice*, the princess was thinking, *should not be in school*. The shoes, which were heeled, pink, and sparkly, were meant to be on ballroom floors or red carpets, not in hallways that smelled like hard-boiled eggs!

"YOU'RE IN GREAT HANDS WITH MISS KINDE!" Principal Fish roared. "BUT I MUST GO NOW. THE CHILDREN ARE COMING!" He took off, practically (but not quite) running. Running broke rule number two in the *Official Rules of Mountain River Valley Elementary*.

"Let me show you and your mom around, Miranda," Miss Kinde said kindly but firmly.

Miranda finally looked up from her feet and walked into the classroom, which, thankfully, didn't smell like anything. QM followed behind her.

"We're going to have a great year," Miss Kinde said. "You're going to love Three B."

Miranda stared at the woman in front of her. She'd never *like* 3B, let alone love it! As Miss Kinde talked about book nooks and science centers, the princess's head began to ache. She glanced out the window at the empty playground. She'd probably have to go out there, she thought, her stomach somersaulting.

Even though Miranda was a kid, she did not enjoy kid things, like monkey bars or ice pops or freeze tag. She liked nail polish, shoes, shoe shopping, arranging furniture, clothes, clothes shopping, rearranging furniture, and planning parties. She also liked being quiet.

Miranda had been perfectly happy with Madame Cornelia, who had been the royal tutor for around a century. Madame Cornelia often forgot to teach things like math or spelling or science. She loved to talk about china patterns and antiques and never noticed if Miranda got up to paint her nails or take a bubble bath during their lessons, which were often about china patterns and antiques. But now Madame Cornelia had decided to retire (to focus on her antique china patterns)!

Miranda knew that soon the empty, quiet playground would fill up with children who would scream and shout. Miranda did not spend much time with children and/or playgrounds, and she didn't want to.

Miranda looked at her mother, but QM was too busy listening to Miss Kinde to notice. The princess rubbed her head and looked out the window again. Just as she had feared, millions of children wearing bright and clashing color combinations were streaming toward the playground. The children wore polka dots, stripes, and plaids and arrived by foot, scooters, and cars. They came by bike and bus. Some little ones cried and tried to hide, while the bigger ones zoomed in, shouting at friends.

*Friends*, the princess thought with a shudder. She'd never have anything to talk about with kids her age. What if they wanted her to do something terrible with them like playing tag or climbing on top of the monkey bars? The princess gulped a mouthful of air.

Miranda watched as Principal Fish walked to the middle of the playground hugging an over-sized clipboard to his chest. When the children on the playground saw him, they scrambled into many crooked lines.

Head and heart and stomach pounding, Miranda looked away from the playground and

over to her teacher. Miss Kinde smiled. "You can take your seat now," she said, pointing to a desk in the back left of the classroom that had a name tag on it that said *Miranda Rose Lapointsetta*. QM walked over to the princess, kissed her on the head, and told her to have a wonderful day.

An extremely loud bell rang out at a terrifying volume. Princess Miranda's heart sank as she dropped into the seat and watched her mother walk away. The princess had never been to school before, but she knew that at any minute a group of loud children would come into the classroom and want to know what in the world she was doing there.

# 3

# MAUDE BRANDYWINE MAYHEW KAYE IS SO HAPPY SHE'S NOT LATE

While Miranda sat frozen at her desk inside 3B, Miss Kinde stepped back into the hard-boiled-eggs-smelling hallway to greet her students. As each child walked inside the classroom, Miss Kinde looked them in the eye, smiled, and said, "Welcome to Three B. Please find your desk and take a seat." Miss Kinde had a lovely, honey-like voice, so it was pleasant to hear her say this fifteen times.

The last person to be greeted by Miss Kinde was out of breath, freckled, and wearing huge rect- angular glasses on top of her head and roller skates over her shoes. She was also the only person who shook Miss Kinde's hand and stopped to chat.

"Hello," the girl said, taking a big gulp of air. "My name is Maude Brandywine Mayhew Kaye. I'm so happy I'm not late on the first day! I can't believe I slept through my rooster!"

Miss Kinde gave the girl a small smile.

"My rooster, General Cockatoo, is my alarm clock. I have ten chickens. Actually eleven. I got a new one last week. Her name is Rosalie, and she's my only Frizzle. She has curly feathers!"

Miss Kinde nodded. "Welcome to Three B, Maude."

"I feel most welcome. Miss Creaky taught me nothing last year," Maude said, pointing down the hall to last year's classroom. "She's probably one hundred and two years old." Maude moved her glasses from her head to her eyes.

Miss Kinde glanced inside 3B. The class was getting noisy, but Maude wasn't done talking.

"I want you to know that I choose to come to school, Miss Kinde. Every year my dad, Walter

Matthews Mayhew Kaye the eighth, asks me and Michael-John, that's my brother, how we plan to learn. I always choose school!"

Miss Kinde smiled.

"Michael-John chooses home school. He stays in his pajamas and reads dictionaries. He knows practically every word. But I want to be a social justice advocate when I grow up. That's someone who makes sure things are equal for all people. So I need to be with The People! I thought about being a farmer, but I had a terrible time with my tomato plant this summer." Maude sighed. "The plant grew and grew, but I didn't get one tomato."

"Tomatoes need lots of sun," Miss Kinde said, shifting on her feet.

"I gave it lots of sunshine!" Maude pushed the glasses back on top of her head and tried to sound passionate and sincere.

"Perhaps we'll study tomatoes," Miss Kinde said. "Now please find your desk and remove your skates. You know they're not allowed in school."

"Rule fifty-eight," Maude recited proudly. "No wearing wheeled shoes on school grounds." She whistled as she skated over to her desk, which was in the back left corner of the room. Maude sat down, removed her skates, and took out a hard-boiled egg and five pencils from the big pockets of her pants. She put everything on her desk in a jumble and waited for something interesting to happen.

When nothing happened, Maude looked around and sighed. Here were all the same kids she'd gone to school with for around three hundred years. None of her classmates had taken their seats yet or asked how her summer had been. Like usual, Agnes and Agatha were giggling. Desdemona was chatting with Norbert, while Fletcher showed Felix his scabby elbow. Over by the Book Nook, a tall boy named Donut was seeing how long he could balance on one leg. Maude's heart sank as she watched the dreadful Hillary Greenlight-Miller put an apple on Miss Kinde's desk.

Hillary Greenlight-Miller had gotten glasses over the summer. Glasses that weren't enormous and seemed to stay on her eyes. Maude put her glasses on her desk and looked at them wistfully. She was only able to wear them for ten seconds at a time. Any longer and she'd feel dizzy, like she might throw up. For years, Maude had wished with all her might that she would need glasses, since all the best social justice revolutionaries wore them. Unfortunately, despite getting many opinions, Maude still had perfect vision. Although she'd missed something right next to her that everyone else in the class had definitely seen.

In addition to hugging and chatting, the other students in 3B were staring at the girl in the left corner of the room who was not Maude. Fletcher, Felix, Desdemona, Norbert, and Hillary Greenlight-Miller, along with everyone else, couldn't help but stare at Princess Miranda. They couldn't believe an actual princess was just sitting there!

Maude and Miss Kinde were the only two people in 3B not buzzing from the excitement of having a princess in class. Miss Kinde loved all children, and Maude, who was busy straightening her wobbly hard-boiled egg, hadn't looked to her right yet.

# 4

# MAUDE LOOKS TO HER RIGHT

When the final morning bell rang, a fly landed on Maude's wrist. She flicked the fly off, causing her to look to her right, and that's when she noticed: Someone was next to her! Someone new! And this new someone, like Maude, was sitting!

Keeping one hand on her wobbly egg, Maude put on her glasses and glanced at the new girl again. How did she know that face?

Miss Kinde stepped to the front of the room. "Class! Let's begin. I'm Miss Kinde—that's kind with a silent *e*. We're going to have a terrific year. First, let's welcome our new classmate. Miranda, welcome to Mountain River Valley. Welcome to Three B."

Maude's glasses slid straight down her nose. *Princess* Miranda? She was sitting next to a princess? No wonder she looked familiar! All her life, Maude had seen pictures and heard stories about the royal family. Whenever they drove by the castle, Maude's dad would dream aloud about all the undiscovered beetles on the property. To Maude Brandywine Mayhew Kaye, Princess Miranda had always seemed like a character in a book, not an actual person. And yet here she was, right next to Maude, just thirteen inches away!

This was an opportunity, Maude thought. Here, finally, was another girl who looked as out of place as Maude felt, even though Maude had been going to Mountain River Valley for around nine million years.

Maude had to seize this opportunity! She looked at the princess. She looked at her egg.

"Would you like a hard-boiled egg?" she asked.

The princess didn't say anything.

*Maybe she didn't hear me*, Maude thought. She picked up her egg. "Would you like this egg?" she asked a little louder, nudging the egg closer to the princess. "It comes from my chickens," she said proudly. "I have eleven chickens. And one rooster named General Cockatoo. That's a funny name, because cockatoos are parrots, not chickens." Maude laughed.

The princess remained quiet and wrinkled her nose.

"I love all animals. But chickens are my favorite. Well, second favorite. My dog, Rudolph Valentino, is the most amazing dog in the universe. But he doesn't lay eggs." Maude laughed again. It would be so great if her dog could lay eggs!

The princess finally turned to look at Maude. Maude grinned as widely as she could.

"Would you like this egg?" Maude asked again.

"No!" the princess said. Her voice wasn't loud, but it was very clear. "Hard-boiled eggs are . . ."

Maude stared at the princess. She hoped the princess might say something like, "Hard-boiled eggs are too delicious to have in school. Why don't we eat them together in the castle, and you can tell me all about your amazing chickens?"

But instead the princess whispered, "Hard-boiled eggs are revolting! They make me want to vomit!"

# 5

# YOU JOURNALS

Maude felt small and weak when Miranda said her egg was revolting. She glared at the princess, who was wearing all pink. *I hate pink*, she thought, as Miss Kinde held up a small blue notebook. *Pink is the worst color in the universe.*

"Class," Miss Kinde said, "this is a You Journal. It's a notebook that's just for you. It should be with you at all times, because you never know when you'll have an amazing idea."

Everyone in 3B groaned except Maude (who loved the idea of a notebook for amazing ideas) and Miranda (who was confused).

Hillary Greenlight-Miller shot up her hand. "Miss Kinde? Will our You Journals be graded? If we write a lot, can we get extra credit?"

Miss Kinde shook her head. "Your You Journals are only for you. No one else should read them."

Hillary Greenlight-Miller frowned, but everyone else seemed pleased. Maude opened her You Journal and immediately drew the following:

Then she drew this:

## 6

# TOTALLY ALONE AT STICKY DESK

Princess Miranda had stopped breathing. Through her nose, that is. She was trying to breathe only with her mouth so she wouldn't have to smell the hideous egg. The owner of the disgusting egg kept putting on and taking off a pair of ugly glasses and was busily writing in her You Journal.

Miranda didn't know what she was supposed to write in the journal. She didn't understand anything Miss Kinde had said. Plus, she didn't have a pencil. But even if she did have a pencil, she wouldn't have known what to write. She hated writing. And reading. And school. And hard-boiled eggs! She felt alone and stared at. Every few minutes, someone else in 3B turned around to look at her.

Miranda didn't mind being stared at when

she walked down a red carpet between QM and KD (King Dad). Safe between her parents, she was happy to give a little wave and a smile. But being stared at in school felt different. In a bad way. The princess felt all alone at her slightly sticky desk and chair.

She looked up at the clock on the wall and was filled with dread. The clock hadn't moved at all! She'd be here for another six and a half hours. Miranda didn't think her first day of school would ever end.

She missed Madame Cornelia and desperately wished something terrible would happen that would let her skip school for the rest of her life (but not something too terrible that would ruin her shoes). She closed her eyes, rubbed her temples, and sniffed. The horrible egg smell was making her headache even worse.

She had known that school would be full of noisy children. She had known that there would be teachers and tests. But she hadn't realized that the grossest food in the universe would be right next to her! *Everyone* knew Miranda hated hard-boiled eggs. How could she be sitting right next to one? Didn't the girl next to her know who she was?

The princess tried not to breathe, but the hard-boiled-egg smell was getting stronger.

Finally, after several centuries passed, a bell rang, and Miranda and the rest of 3B left the classroom and went to a horrible smelly place where they were told to eat. But Miranda couldn't eat, even though the castle chef had packed her favorite cheeses, along with fresh croissants and fruit.

After that, 3B went to another loud and smelly room where a woman laughed as she hurled balls over some kind of net. Finally, 3B went back to 3B, where Miss Kinde told them a million things about after-school clubs, and then about three million rules were announced over the loudspeaker. Then, finally-finally, the dismissal bell rang.

Miranda dragged her aching feet and head down the long hallway, out of school, and over to the carpool lane, where Blake had parked the fancy automobile.

"That goes against rule number forty-nine," she heard a voice call from above.

The princess looked up and saw the hard-boiled-egg girl sitting in a tree.

"According to the *Official Rules of Mountain River Valley Elementary*, cars can't *park* in the carpool lane. And they can't pick up one child."

Miranda ignored Maude and crawled into the back seat of the royal automobile.

She had done it.

She'd gone to school for an entire day.

She only hoped she wouldn't have to do it ever again.

## 7

# UP A TREE

Even though it went against rule number ninety-seven, Maude was sitting up in the oak tree in front of school. Principal Fish was so busy dealing with students who had broken first day rules (running, chewing gum, spitting, running while chewing gum and spitting) that she figured she'd get away with it.

It was a sunny afternoon, and Maude was happy to be outside, but she was getting hungry watching the jump-roping club eat ice pops over in the playground. Behind them, the gardening club munched veggies. Maude took out a small pair of binoculars from her pants and focused them on the gardening club's tomato plants. There were lots of tomatoes growing on the vines.

*No fair*, she thought. *Why didn't my plant grow tomatoes?* She would have liked to ask the gardening club gardeners, but Hillary Greenlight-Miller was president, and Maude didn't spend any more time with Hillary than she had to. How annoying that Hillary got to wear glasses and eat homegrown tomatoes even though she didn't really like gardening. Hillary just liked being president, which was why, in addition to the gardening club, she was president of the marbles club, the yo-yo club, the homework club, and the practice Mandatory National Reading and Writing and Math Exam club, of which she was the only member. Maude wasn't in any clubs, because Hillary was in all of them.

But still, Maude thought, even with her arch-nemesis Hillary Greenlight-Miller, 3B seemed much better than 2L. When Maude got home, she'd tell her dad and brother just that. Then her brother would define a word she didn't know, and her dad would ask her if she'd learned anything. Maude closed her eyes in thought. Miss Kinde was nice, and she really liked her You Journal, but Maude couldn't think of anything she'd learned. Her classmates still weren't interested in anything she liked, and not one of them had asked her what she'd done over summer vacation.

Her stomach growled. *I learned that one hard-boiled egg isn't nearly enough lunch*, she thought. Then Maude remembered how Princess Miranda had said hard-boiled eggs were revolting. Maude opened her eyes. She *had* learned something! She'd learned that princesses were rude!

Rudeness was a kind of injustice, Maude thought. Rudeness shouldn't be tolerated! Feeling

motivated, Maude packed up her binoculars, swung herself out of the tree, and roller-skated home in a record-breaking six minutes.

When Maude got home, she took off her skates, climbed up twenty-seven slightly crooked stairs, and burst into her house. "You're never going to believe it!" she called.

"I always believe you, Maude," her dad said. Her dad, Walter Matthews Mayhew Kaye VIII, was doing a headstand, as he'd been when she'd left him that morning. Maude's dad had many interests, including yoga, beetles, juggling, soup making, and reciting quotes to his children every morning.

Maude's brother, Michael-John, was also where she'd left him, which was in sheep pajamas, hunched over a stack of dictionaries.

"There's a princess in my class this year," Maude announced, petting Rudolph Valentino, her beloved dog.

Walt lowered his left leg, Michael-John turned to page 802 in a musty dictionary, and Rudolph Valentino yawned, then farted.

"Do you want a snack, my little mountain pine beetle? There's some cheese on the counter."

Maude looked at her father and then her brother, who was still reading. "Did you hear me say there's a princess in my class? An actual, real-life princess. She sits next to me since we're in alphabetical order."

"I heard you." Walt lowered his right leg. "William Shakespeare wrote, 'My crown is in my heart, not on my head.' Does your princess wear a crown?" He flipped so he was suddenly sitting cross-legged in front of Maude.

"She's not *my* princess," Maude told him. "And no, she wasn't wearing a crown. Just loads of pink, which I learned is the worst color in the world."

Walt smiled. "That's a matter of opinion. I like pink. So, my coconut rhinoceros beetle, have you and the real-life pink princess become friends?"

Maude stared at her father. For someone who knew so much about so many things, he was totally bananas. "No," she said. "I have absolutely, positively *not* become friends with the princess." *And I never will*, she thought.

## 8

# WHEN MIRANDA GOT HOME

When Miranda slowly walked into the castle, QM and KD were waiting in the entryway.

"How was the first day, darling?" QM asked eagerly.

"What did you learn?" KD asked. "Tell me one thing."

"Did you make friends? Is your teacher nice?" QM asked.

"Did you have enough to eat?" KD smiled at her.

Staring at her parents in their fancy clothes, Miranda realized there were not enough words in her vocabulary to describe her first day of school. How could she explain all the rules? Or how often and loudly the bells rang? What about the way the children in 3B stared at her? And, perhaps most strange of all, how she, Princess Miranda, known hater of hard-boiled eggs, had been offered a hard-boiled egg! How could she explain all this?

"There . . ." Miranda choked out. "There was . . ."

QM and KD smiled eagerly.

"THERE WAS A HARD-BOILED EGG!" Miranda shouted. Then she ran past her parents, through several long hallways, and up several spiraling staircases, before entering her wing and collapsing on her enormous, perfectly made bed.

The princess stayed in bed for the rest of the day. And the night. She wished, more than anything, that she could stay there forever. Unfortunately, just after sunrise, her parents rushed in.

"Good morning, sunshine!" QM beamed.

"It's the second day of school!" KD shouted happily.

"I can't get up," the princess said. Even though she'd been in bed for many hours, she hadn't slept and felt tired. And miserable.

"Of course you can get out of bed," KD said cheerfully.

The princess shook her head. "I'm sick."

QM put her hand on her daughter's forehead.

"It's my stomach," the princess said. "And my head."

"You're going to school, Miranda," KD told her.

"Can't Madame Cornelia come back?" Miranda begged. "She could give me homework."

"No," QM said. "Madame Cornelia finally retired. She's not coming back."

The princess scowled.

"Your father and I have come to believe that school is better than having a royal tutor come here." QM looked at all the fabulous things in her daughter's room. There was the Victorian dollhouse that was big enough for Miranda to stand in, a hammock suspended from the ceiling, a ninety-inch pink television set, and a wall of very organized nail polishes. "It's good for you to spend time out of the castle with people your own age."

Miranda rolled onto her side and looked at the pink wall. People her age? People her age didn't know the difference between the color chartreuse and the color cerulean! If her endless first day of school had taught her anything, it was that people her age wore ugly shoes, chewed gum, and talked with their mouths full.

Not that they talked to her. They just stared at her and then whispered and giggled. Normally, being a princess made Miranda feel different in a special way, but yesterday she had just felt different in a weird way. Why didn't anyone else jump when the loud bells rang? What was the Mandatory National Reading and Writing and Math Exam, and why did everyone in 3B groan every time Miss Kinde mentioned it? She didn't understand what the kids talked about either. What was an allowance? And why on earth would anyone have a pet chicken?

*Chickens*, the princess thought with a shudder. Chickens laid eggs! Spending time with people her age meant spending time with people like the hard-boiled-egg girl!

"I can't go to school," she moaned.

"Of course you can," said KD. "Why couldn't you?"

"It smells," the princess said. "And it gives me a terrible headache."

QM lifted the pink blanket off of the princess.

"Up and at 'em, Miranda," KD commanded. "You're going back to school."

# 9

# MIRANDA GOES BACK TO SCHOOL

The second day at Mountain River Valley began with an assembly, during which experts expertly explained the best way for students to bubble in the green answer sheets for the practice Mandatory National Reading and Writing and Math Exams they would take all year.

For everyone except Hillary Greenlight-Miller, the assembly, like the exam, was painful and boring. Princess Miranda did not understand a word, and Maude spent most of the time looking for her You Journal in her messy messenger bag. When she finally found it, she doodled this:

After the assembly, 3B walked back to 3B, which was stuffy and warm. Miss Kinde passed out long sheets of green paper and thick test booklets and opened the classroom windows. Miranda was grateful for the fresh air, but then Maude put three pencils, a long feather, and *two* hard-boiled eggs on her desk!

Miranda gasped.

Miss Kinde, thinking the princess was concerned about the test, ran over. "This is a Mandatory National Reading and Writing and Math Exam," she explained.

The princess rubbed her aching head.

"Don't worry," her teacher said. "It's only a practice test. You'll take many practice exams." She sighed as if this made her very sad. "The real exam is at the end of the year."

The princess nodded, although she knew she wouldn't make it to the end of her second *day*, let alone the end of the *year*.

"Just do as well as you can," Miss Kinde added.

"I don't have a pencil," the princess said quietly.

"Oh." Miss Kinde looked around, her eyes stopping on Maude. "Maude, may Miranda borrow a pencil?"

Maude scowled but handed one to the princess.

"You may begin, class," Miss Kinde said.

While 3B bubbled in their ovals, the classroom lights flickered, and Miranda's head pounded. Just reading the questions made her so tired and weak that she could barely hold Maude's terrible pencil. The point was so dull that Miranda had to use all the energy in her hand to fill an oval. And she soon discovered that the pencil had barely any eraser, so when she tried to erase answer three, the sheet ripped.

Then a gentle breeze breezed into 3B and swept the hard-boiled-egg smell right into Miranda's nose. She closed her eyes. Two hard-boiled eggs were so much smellier than one.

The princess opened her eyes and glanced at the hard-boiled-egg girl. Maude's test booklet was closed, and she was writing in her You Journal.

Miranda's heart sank. How could Maude be

done already? Miranda had about eight hundred more questions to bubble in. And what was Maude writing? Miranda hadn't written a single word in her stupid You Journal.

Another breeze forced so much hard-boiled-egg smell into the princess's nose that she sneezed, very loudly, three times in a row. The class turned to look at her. She sneezed again, and her eyes began to water. She couldn't hate hard-boiled eggs any more!

Something orange landed on her desk. The princess stared at it. She was afraid to touch it because it was covered with sticky bits and some kind of fur.

"It's a handkerchief," Maude whispered. "You can use it."

Miranda shook her head, which made her nose drip.

"You don't want my handkerchief?" Maude hissed.

"No," the princess muttered. She thought of her collection of handkerchiefs back in the castle. They were clean, and silk, and, thanks to Madame Cornelia's instruction, folded into perfect triangles! Now *those* were handkerchiefs!

"Your nose is dripping, but you won't use my handkerchief, even though it was in the famous War of Jenkin's Ear?"

"Class, you have three minutes left," Miss Kinde announced.

*Three minutes*, the princess thought. *Three minutes to get through eight hundred questions.*

"Are you too good to use my handkerchief?" Maude whispered.

*What does good have to do with it?* Miranda wondered. She just wanted to be left alone in her wing of the castle for the rest of her life. The princess closed her eyes and pictured her beautiful, quiet room. She missed her shoes, her closets, and all of her nail polishes. She missed all the time she used to have to organize her things and arrange her furniture. She sneezed again. And again. And again. If only she'd brought a real handkerchief! And a gallon of perfume.

"Do you think you're better than me because I'm just a humble social justice activist?" Maude asked.

Miranda didn't understand Maude's question or any of the questions on the practice exam. She didn't know why someone would put hard-boiled eggs on their desk or get mad when someone else didn't want to use a filthy bandana.

"One minute remaining," Miss Kinde said sweetly.

Except for Maude and Miranda, all the other kids in 3B quickly finished filling in their ovals. Tears welled in the princess's eyes as she looked at her nearly blank answer sheet. She had no answers.

"Well?" Maude asked.

"It smells," Miranda said finally. "The bandana

smells and so do your rotten eggs! Isn't there a rule about hard-boiled eggs in school?"

"No!" Maude said. "There is no rule about eggs!" With that, she grabbed her handkerchief and stuffed it into her pocket.

Princess Miranda breathed a small sigh of relief. Then she looked down at her practice Mandatory National Reading and Writing and Math Exam and felt miserable all over again.

# 10

# DAY THREE AT MOUNTAIN RIVER VALLEY ELEMENTARY

Maude (who had stayed up late reading about growing tomatoes) and Miranda (who couldn't fall asleep on school nights) were both tired on the third day of school. But that was the only similar thing.

Maude wore an orange shirt that said FIGHT THE POWER, her dirty brown cargo pants, two different colored socks, and combat boots.

Miranda wore gold wedge shoes and a very shiny pink pantsuit.

When the bell rang, Maude (who had overslept again) rushed to her desk and set out her You Journal, three hard-boiled eggs, her harmonica, and five pencils.

Miranda put some things on her desk, too. She still hadn't found a pencil, but she'd brought a small pink candle, a diamond box of tissues, and a doily to cover her desk. She lined everything up in a very neat row.

"You can't light that candle," Maude told her. "It breaks rule seventy-seven. No burning sticks, leaves, homework, metal, or *candles* on school grounds."

"I'm not going to burn it," Miranda said quietly. "I just smell it." She picked the candle up and breathed in the sweet smell of "violets in the rain." If she kept her nose on the candle and closed her eyes, she could almost pretend she didn't smell the revolting hard-boiled eggs.

# 11

# DAY FOUR AT MOUNTAIN RIVER VALLEY ELEMENTARY

On the fourth day at Mountain River Valley, Maude brought in four hard-boiled eggs, her orange handkerchief, a rusty harmonica, a set of yellow false teeth, a snakeskin, and a miniature ship in a bottle.

Miranda brought in her doily, two pink candles, the tissues in the diamond box, and a small bottle of nail polish called "pinktastically pink."

## 12

# FRIDAY AT MOUNTAIN RIVER VALLEY ELEMENTARY

On the fifth day of school, Maude put a piece of blue cheese, eight pencils, the rusty harmonica, the orange handkerchief, the false teeth, and the snakeskin on her desk. There was so much stuff, the desk was barely visible, but then she reached into her green canvas bag and took out *six* hard-boiled eggs! She lined them up in a crooked row.

Next to her, Miranda reached into her fancy leather bag and set up, in neat rows, three candles, the doily, a small oval mirror, four bottles of nail polish, and a shiny ruby pen, because she still couldn't find a pencil anywhere in the castle.

It was the pen that brought everything to an end.

It was so shiny and sparkly that everyone in 3B, even Miss Kinde, kept looking at it.

"That is a lovely pen, Miranda," Miss Kinde said right before giving out yet another practice Mandatory National Reading and Writing and Math Exam. "But very distracting."

"Hard-boiled eggs are distracting, too," Miranda whispered, because she wasn't used to talking in class.

"Excuse me?" Miss Kinde said.

The princess felt too shy to repeat what she had said, but Hillary Greenlight-Miller, who had amazing hearing, yelled, "She said, 'Hard-boiled eggs are distracting, too,' Miss Kinde!"

In one second, thirty eyes were on Maude.

Maude scrunched her face. *There's nothing wrong with hard-boiled eggs*, she told herself. There was no rule against them!

"Maude?" Miss Kinde walked over to Maude's

desk. "Why do you have six hard-boiled eggs on your desk?"

"They're from my amazing chickens," Maude said, trying to sound proud. "I collect their eggs every morning. After I sing to them. There's no rule in the *Official Rules of Mountain River Valley Elementary* about hard-boiled eggs!"

Miss Kinde looked at Maude and her eggs, then at Miranda, then back at Maude's eggs. Finally, she said, "No, there's no rule against having hard-boiled eggs in school, but since lunch isn't for several hours, please put your eggs in your lunch bag."

"Maude always eats gross food," Hillary Greenlight-Miller announced.

"School lunches are grosser," Maude said to Hillary Greenlight-Miller.

Miranda couldn't help but nod as she watched Maude and Hillary stick their tongues out at each other. School lunches looked absolutely disgusting. It was all she could do to choke down a few bites of her own lunch, since the cafeteria smelled almost as bad as the gym and was as loud as the music room.

"Girls," Miss Kinde said, "there'll be no more discussion of lunch. Maude, put your eggs away."

"Do I have to? It's not in the *Official*—"

"It's a *class* rule," Miss Kinde said quickly. "Put the harmonica away, too. And the snakeskin, the cheese, and false teeth. You don't want distractions while taking the practice Mandatory National Reading and Writing and Math Exam."

"I'm not distracted," Maude grumbled, putting her things back in her bag. "I always get the highest score on the practice Mandatory National Reading and Writing and Math Exam."

She looked right at Hillary Greenlight-Miller, who stuck her tongue back out.

Princess Miranda sneezed and took one of the tissues out of the diamond box.

Maude pointed to the princess. "How come *she* gets to have stuff on her desk? Because she's a princess?"

It felt strange to hear Maude call her a princess, Miranda thought. Until that moment she wasn't sure Maude actually knew she was royal. Who would offer a princess a dirty handkerchief, dull pencils, or hard-boiled eggs?

Miss Kinde looked at all the things that were lined up on Miranda's desk. Then she cleared her throat. "Class," she said, "starting today, all personal items will be kept in your backpacks."

"Maude doesn't have a backpack," Hillary Greenlight-Miller said. "Just her ugly green sack."

"Hey!" Maude scowled at Hillary. "That bag belonged to my great-great-great-grandfather. With only eighteen cents and a one-eyed cat named Onion the Great, he explored the world on a unicycle!"

"Ewww," Hillary said. "One-eyed cats are the worst."

Maude scowled at Hillary. "My cat, Onion the Great Number Eleven, is lovely! But not as lovely as Rudolph Valentino, my dog."

"Animals belong in zoos," Hillary Greenlight-Miller said, straightening her glasses.

Maude gasped.

"Girls!" Miss Kinde said sharply. "Please, we must start the practice exam."

*I don't have a backpack either*, Miranda thought as she put her wonderful pen and candles and tissues in her fancy leather bag.

As Miss Kinde handed out the green paper with all the ovals, Maude glared at Miranda. "This is your fault," she said.

"What did I do?" Miranda whispered. "Miss Kinde made a new rule."

Maude looked at the princess. It was that sparkly pen that had caused her eggs and snakeskin and harmonica to be banned. *It wasn't fair*, she thought. *Why should Miranda and her stupid pen have so much power?*

# 13

# BREAKFAST WITH KD AND QM

On Monday morning, the princess was miserable and tired. She'd spent the weekend trying to forget Mountain River Valley Elementary by re-arranging a bunch of toys she didn't play with anymore and painting her toenails a dozen different times. But now it was the beginning of the week all over again, and she couldn't stop yawning as she ate her breakfast.

QM leaned across the long table and said, "Why Miranda, your birthday is just two weeks away!"

KD sat upright. "My mashed potatoes! How did we not remember?"

"Miranda has been busy." QM sounded pleased.

Miranda swallowed. Her birthday was in two weeks? She couldn't believe it! All the time she was wasting in school when she could have been party planning! Miranda always threw fantastic birthday parties and, until now, she'd always planned them weeks in advance. School was really getting in the way of all the things she liked to do.

"We'll pull out all the stops," KD said, "since this year's party will be different."

Princess Miranda looked at her dad. Her birthday parties were always incredible. Last year's party included a rocket launch, hot-air balloon rides, and a famous mariachi band. One year, there was a dolphin show. Every year, at the end of the party, fireworks spelled out HAPPY BIRTHDAY, MIRANDA! in bright pink explosions. Why would this year be different?

"This year," KD boomed, "Three B will be here!"

Miranda stared at her father.

"Why bother with the royal children of our royal friends when you have your very own classmates?" KD smiled at his excellent idea. Because Miranda didn't have any friends her age, the guests at her birthday parties had always been the children of the royal people QM and KD knew. Miranda never knew the tiny earls or teen-age dukes at her parties, but she didn't care. She just liked the planning part anyway.

"What a lovely way to meet Three B!" QM said.

"No," the princess said.

Her parents stared at her, which reminded her of all the staring the kids in 3B would be doing in school later that morning. "I can't invite Three B to my party," she told them.

"Why not?" KD asked.

Miranda looked up at the diamond chandelier above her. It was the perfect chandelier for the room, and she had chosen it because she was good at things like that. She understood how lights and tables should look in a room this big. Her parents didn't understand things like that and they wouldn't understand anything about 3B—certainly not how, just after Miss Kinde had said the new rule about how all home things had to be left in bags, the boy two seats in front of her, Fletcher, had asked for a pencil. He was talking to Maude, but since he was staring at Miranda, she accidentally handed him the ruby pen from her bag. Fletcher said something about pens on practice exams breaking rule number forty-two, which made her realize that the pen wasn't even supposed to be out of her bag! In a panic, she'd grabbed it, only to watch Maude hand Fletcher one of her sticky pencils.

Later, at recess, which was noisier than PE and lunch and music combined, Agatha had said she liked Miranda's sweater.

The princess had nodded.

"I love it!" Agatha had said, stepping closer to touch it. "Did you get it at Tops and Tees?"

Miranda shook her head.

"Pants and Pullovers?" Agatha asked.

Miranda had never heard of Tops and Tees or Pants and Pullovers, but she guessed they were clothing stores. She shook her head, hoping Agatha would go back to chasing Donut around the playground, but Agatha had stayed put.

"Where did you get it? I'd love one!"

Miranda didn't know how to tell Agatha about Yoshi von Mutter, the world-famous fashion designer, and his assistant tailor Starbella Loon. Four times a year, Yoshi and Starbella came to the castle to outfit the royal family for the upcoming season. For nearly a week, Miranda and Yoshi pored over magazines and swaths of the fanciest French fabrics. Yoshi would stay up every night cutting and trimming and measuring and sticking all kinds of pins in all kinds of places. At the end of the week, the royal family had exquisite one-of-a-kind wardrobes, and Yoshi and Starbella would jet off to their next royal family.

How could Miranda describe all this to Agatha? "I don't know . . ." she'd finally said. "It was in one of my closets."

Agatha had given her a weird look and walked away.

"Your class would love to come to your birthday party," QM said, jolting Miranda back to the breakfast table.

"No, they wouldn't," Miranda whispered.

"Of course they would." KD chuckled. "We'll borrow a lion! A white lion! Won't that be something?"

"I don't think they'd like it," Miranda said. "I don't think Three B will want to come to my party."

KD and QM laughed. "It's your birthday party!" KD said. "At our castle! What could they possibly not like?"

*Me*, Miranda thought. *They could not like me.*

## 14

# THE INVITATIONS

But in the same way they'd decided that she was going to school, QM and KD decided that Miranda would take the dusted-with-gold invitations with her on her eighth day at Mountain River Valley Elementary.

When Miranda got to school early for her extra-extra Mandatory National Reading and Writing and Math Exam practice, Miss Kinde handed her a test and told her to get started while she went to make copies. Because the other students didn't need extra-extra practice, Miranda was alone.

Instead of starting her practice exam, Miranda took the invitations out of her bag, took a deep breath, and began putting them on desks. One invitation for Agatha and another for Agnes. She put an invitation on Donut's desk, then one on Norbert's, and another one on Norris's. She went to the next row and put one on Fletcher's desk and, pausing for a minute, one on Hillary Greenlight-Miller's. She kept going until she got to Maude's desk, which was empty except for a sticky spot in the middle, three pencils, and her You Journal. Miranda thought it still smelled like hard-boiled eggs.

She held her nose and lowered the invitation just as a breeze came through the open window. The breeze opened Maude's You Journal to the very first page, and the princess couldn't believe what she saw. Maude was drawing! Not writing! Drawing! Miranda saw the picture of a dreadful dog and a smiling Miss Kinde and the hard-boiled eggs.

And then she saw the pictures of her!

There was an enormous crown on top of her head! She'd never wear a crown to school. She didn't even like wearing them at royal events. They were heavy and made her head itch. Miranda turned the page and saw another drawing of her wearing shoes that looked like forks! Miranda turned the page and saw the worst drawing of all: She was holding her ruby pen and saying,

Miranda shut her eyes tightly and took a deep breath. Then she opened her eyes to make sure she was still alone. And then Princess Miranda shoved Maude's invitation back into her bag, sat down, and began her practice exam.

## 15

# WHEN MISS KINDE CAME BACK IN

Miss Kinde noticed the invitations as soon as she walked back into 3B. Since rule number eighty-seven in the *Official Rules of Mountain River Valley Elementary* stated that invitations had to be given to everyone in the class, Miss Kinde scanned the room to make certain there was a gold envelope on every desk. She saw envelopes on Agatha's, Norbert's, Fletcher's, and Felix's desks. Hillary Greenlight-Miller had one, too. And Agnes and Donut and Desdemona. But just as Miss Kinde was about to check Maude's desk, Miranda sneezed seven times in a row.

Miss Kinde looked up. "Do you need a tissue?"

Miranda shook her head and pulled out a tissue from the diamond box in her bag. As she took it, her hand grazed the last birthday invitation. Miranda looked at Maude's desk and then at her teacher. But Miss Kinde was frantically stapling practice exams, so Miranda blew her nose and reread question three.

# 16

# WHEN 3B CAME IN

When 3B trooped in, they were heartbroken to see another practice exam, but delighted to see the shiny gold envelopes on their desks. Moving the exams aside, 3B ripped open their invitations:

### HER ROYAL MAJESTY PRINCESS MIRANDA INVITES YOU TO HER BIRTHDAY PARTY

#### SATURDAY, OCTOBER 1 NOON TO MIDNIGHT

HOT-AIR BALLOON RIDES, FASHION SHOW, CASTLE TOURS, TRAMPOLINES, OLYMPIC SOCCER, ELEPHANT RIDES, KARAOKE, SPA TREATMENTS, LIFE-SIZE PIÑATAS, ATV RIDES, BUILD YOUR OWN SUNDAE WITH NOT-YET-INVENTED ICE CREAM, MOVIES IN THE MOVIE THEATER, DONUTS, BOWLING, SWIMMING, MOON VIEWING WITH THE HUBBLE TELESCOPE, FIREWORKS, AND WHITE LION VIEWING.

A LEGAL GUARDIAN MUST SIGN THE WAIVER IN ORDER FOR YOU TO PARTICIPATE IN ANYTHING DANGEROUS.

As her classmates whispered and giggled and smiled big smiles at the princess, Maude, who had almost been late, moved her practice exam to the side to see if her envelope was under it. It wasn't. Maude looked under her desk, but nothing was on the floor. She scowled but didn't say anything. Instead, she opened her You Journal and began to write.

*She's probably drawing another mean picture of me*, the princess thought, *so it's only fair that I didn't invite her.*

# WHAT MAUDE WROTE IN HER YOU JOURNAL

- birthday parties are STUPID!
- I hate birthday parties
- princesses are STUPID!
- I hate princesses

# SUPER RARE IS SUPER COOL

3B couldn't stop chatting about the princess's party. No one in 3B had been to a party that lasted till the next day! In a castle!

"Is there really going to be a white lion?" Norbert asked the princess as 3B made their way to the cafeteria. "White lions are super rare."

"It's being flown in," the princess said, trying not to smell the day's lunch. "From . . . Belgrade." She was pretty sure that was what KD had said.

"Cool," Norbert said. "Super cool!"

*It is cool*, Miranda thought.

During lunch, Agatha and Agnes walked over to the princess.

"Will there really be a fashion show?" Agatha asked.

The princess nodded and tried not to look at their school lunches.

"With fancy clothes?" Agnes looked interested.

Miranda nodded again and tried not to notice Maude slowly nibbling her hard-boiled egg.

As soon as Agnes and Agatha went back to their seats, Donut slid over to the princess. "There'll be doughnuts? At your party?" he asked, then licked his lips.

Miranda didn't remember anything about doughnuts.

"It said doughnuts on the invitation," Donut said.

"Oh." The princess yawned. "There'll be dough-nuts then. Plus cakes, cookies, pies, an ice cream bar, and candy." Miranda yawned again. School made her so very tired. And her head always ached.

"I just care about the doughnuts." Donut drooled onto the gloppy gray food on his tray. "I really love doughnuts."

"Okay," Miranda said, accidently looking at Maude, who was now reading a book called *Revenge Is a Dish Best Served Cold.*

At the end of the eighth day of school, like all
the other days, Miranda was still exhausted, confused, and headachy. But one thing had changed.
While the students in 3B were still staring at her,
all of them (except one) were now smiling at her,
too.

# 19

# PICTURES ON THE WALL

After the dismissal bell rang on the eighth day of school, Maude walked home, ignored her happily clucking chickens, dragged herself up the twenty-seven stairs, and flung herself onto her bed, where she stared at the ceiling. A group of famous revolutionaries that she'd drawn stared back.

Elizabeth Freeman
1742-1829

Helen Keller
1880-1968

Josefina Fierro de Bright
1920-1998

"Did any of you famous revolutionaries ever not get invited to a party?" she asked.

Because they were pictures of people who had died long ago, they didn't answer.

Maude turned onto her side and looked at a framed photograph of a woman holding a baby.

"I miss you, Mom," she said. "If you were alive, I might tell you how I didn't get an invitation to the stupid princess's party. Everyone else got one. Even my archenemy Hillary Greenlight-Miller." Maude touched the picture with her index finger. "I could file an official complaint with Principal Fish. The princess totally broke rule eighty-seven. But . . . I don't want to tell the principal." She picked up a stuffed ladybug. "If I tell Miss Kinde, she'll just feel sorry for me. That's not what I want."

*What do you want?* Maude imagined her mother asking.

She closed her eyes and imagined Principal Fish booming that rule 9,999 was that royalty would no longer be allowed at school. *No,* Maude thought. That would never be a rule. She opened her eyes.

*Did you learn anything today?* Maude imagined her dad asking.

*Well, I learned that it feels awful to not get invited to something even if you don't want to go. I learned that all it takes for my classmates to be friends with someone rude is an invitation to pet a white lion. It isn't fair. The princess should learn something, too.*

*Yes, that's it!* Maude thought with a jolt. *The princess should be taught a lesson!*

And who better to teach her than Maude?

## 20

# A NOUN OR A VERB

That night Maude had a wonderful dream involving protest songs and spray paint, and when she woke up the next morning, she was eager to begin the ninth day of school.

"What's it called when a bunch of people decide not to do something?" she asked her dad and brother over breakfast.

"A boycott?" Walt asked, putting a spoonful of scrambled eggs on Maude's plate.

"Yes!" Maude grinned.

"Boycott can be a noun or a verb," Michael-John said.

"How do you boycott?" Maude asked.

"You have to get a large number of people to stop doing something all together," Michael-John explained.

Maude smiled. A boycott would be the perfect lesson to teach the pink princess. Miranda would definitely learn a lesson if no one went to her party! But how could Maude convince 3B not to go when that was all they talked about?

Maude spent hours jotting down notes in her You Journal. Here are the ideas she came up with:

## BIRTHDAY PARTY BOYCOTT IDEAS

Tell 3B aliens have taken over the castle.
Tell 3B there's bubonic plague at the castle.
Pay 3B not to go to the party.

She also drew a lot of pictures:

## 21

# HELP FROM
# MICHAEL-JOHN

When Maude got home from school on Friday, Walt was nowhere to be seen.

"Where's Dad?" she asked Michael-John, who was actually not in pajamas for once but was still hunched over his dictionaries.

"Beetle symposium. He'll be home for *cena*, which I just learned is Latin for dinner."

"Wasn't he just at a beetle conference?"

Michael-John nodded, but didn't look up. "There are a lot of beetles. And this is a symposium. Last week was a conference."

Maude sat in front of his stack of dictionaries. "I need your help. I'm having a boycott!"

"What are you boycotting?"

"Princess Miranda's birthday party."

"Why?"

"Well, she broke rule eighty-seven in the

*Official Rules of Mountain River Valley Elementary.*"
She petted Onion the Great Number Eleven. "Rule eighty-seven says if you give out invitations during school hours, you have to give one to everyone."

"And you didn't get one?"

Maude shook her head.

"Maybe you lost yours? You lose a lot of things."

"I might not be that organized, but even I can't lose something I never had." Maude took out her You Journal, which was strangely gummy. "The invitations were on *fourteen* desks. Not on mine. I looked. Everywhere."

"Oh."

"I'm tired of writing official letters of complaint to Principal Fish. He never answers. So, I'm going to have a boycott."

"You need numbers to boycott."

"I know! I'm going to get Three B to boycott, too. It's going to be my first official social justice movement!" She found her list in her You Journal and read him her three ideas.

"Those are all terrible ideas," her brother said. "First, no one will believe you about the aliens. If they do, it might make them want to go more. I'd *only* go to a princess party if there were aliens."

Maude nodded in sad agreement.

"And everyone knows that bubonic plague stopped being a real problem in 1959."

"Shucks," Maude said. "What about my last idea?"

"How much money do you have?"

Maude closed her eyes. "Nine dollars and seventeen cents."

Michael-John tapped his fingers on top of a dictionary. "That's about sixty-five cents per person."

Maude sighed.

"Oh well." Michael-John looked back at his dictionary.

Maude put on her glasses. "I need help! Please Michael-John! I need to boycott!"

"Why?"

"The princess is mean," Maude said. "She goes to school super early even though it's against school rules." She took her glasses off.

"You always say you want to get to school early. But then you oversleep and race around putting weird stuff in your pockets and end up late."

"It's not weird stuff," Maude said. "It's all the stuff I need for school."

"Maybe the princess goes to school early for extra help."

Maude ignored this possibility. "Well, it was her stupid ruby pen that got my hard-boiled eggs taken away and she never eats the school food or plays her recorder at music and she just stands there at PE and recess."

"Do you play the recorder?" Michael-John asked.

"Of course not! School recorders are gross.

And my harmonica sounds much better." Luckily Mr. Mancini, the music teacher, was around 182 years old and hadn't yet noticed her harmonica.

"You don't eat school food either," Michael-John said. "You bring your lunch."

"Not from a castle."

"You don't live in a castle."

"NO," Maude screeched. "I DON'T!"

"If you lived in a castle, you'd probably be a princess."

"I'm absolutely not a princess!"

Michael-John nodded calmly. "But if you were a princess, you'd bring your lunch from your castle."

Maude scowled. "I bring lunch from home, because Principal Fish still won't do anything about the Styrofoam lunch trays. You're not helping, Michael-John. How do I get Three B to join my boycott?"

"What about the truth?"

*The truth*, Maude thought. *The truth*? Should she tell 3B about the hard-boiled eggs and the bandana and how she was the only one in the whole class not to get invited?

It was so simple! Truth! Just five little letters. Could she do it? Could Maude Brandywine Mayhew Kaye, the roller-skating social justice revolutionary of Mountain River Valley Elementary, tell the truth?

# 22

# MAUDE
# TELLS THE TRUTH

The next day was Saturday, which meant there was just one week before Princess Miranda's birthday party extravaganza. For the first time ever, Maude woke before her rooster crowed. She felt ready to tell the truth and organize a boycott!

She wore her JUSTICE FOR ALL sweatshirt, cargo pants, and VOTES FOR WOMEN sash. She tied the orange bandana around her head and put two pencils, her harmonica, a compass, three Band-Aids, and a small pack of ancient Rainbow Sweeties into her pockets. Then she stomped into the living room.

"I leave now, for Justice!" she told her dad, who was on his head, and her brother, who was reading the definition of the noun *fair shake*.

"*Fair shake* means fair chance or treatment," Michael-John said. "It was first used in 1930."

"Peace is its own reward," Walt said.

"I'm busy," Maude replied. "I don't have time for quotes or definitions, gentlemen."

"There's always time for quotes," Walt said. "Mahatma Gandhi once said, 'Peace is its own reward.' Do you know who he was?"

"He freed India from British rule," Maude said, putting two hard-boiled eggs into her last empty pocket.

"Yes. Mahatma Gandhi inspired movements for freedom around the world."

"I'm not sure when I'll be home."

"Be home by three, my lovely leaf beetle."

"I'll try," Maude said, strapping on her skates.

Using Mountain River Valley's official school directory, Maude found her classmates' addresses. She rang doorbells, buzzed buzzers, and knocked on doors with heavy brass knockers. And, when her classmates weren't home, Maude found them at soccer games, origami instruction, and indoor swimming pools. Maude's classmates thought it was strange that Maude had found them on a Saturday, but they also liked it. It made them feel special to have Maude skate over and say, "I must talk to you about something important!" With each classmate, Maude would take a deep breath and tell them how rude the princess had been about the hard-boiled egg and handkerchief.

Most of Maude's classmates thought it was super weird that Maude had offered the princess a hard-boiled egg. They also thought it was unusual that Maude had given the princess a handkerchief when there were boxes and boxes of tissues in 3B. And most of them just nodded as Maude talked about famous boycotts and social justice movements in history. But when she told them the real and painful truth, they all listened.

"The real and painful truth," Maude would say to Norbert or Agatha or whomever she was talking to, "is that Princess Miranda did not invite me to her birthday party."

Whomever Maude was talking to would look shocked.

"There was an invitation on everyone's desk. Except mine!"

"Really?" Fletcher or Felix or Desdemona would ask.

"Really! And even though I know it breaks rule eighty-seven, I'm not here about the rules. I'm here because the next time the princess has a party, she might not invite . . . you!"

Maude enjoyed watching the person across from her think about this. When it was clear they understood, she would take out her You Journal and have them sign under her Birthday Boycott Pledge with numbers one to fifteen. She had signed on the first line, and as she went from house to apartment building to soccer field, she filled up all the other lines, until there were just two more lines left to fill.

Unfortunately, the second-to-last person Maude needed to sign the Birthday Boycott Pledge was the annoying Hillary Greenlight-Miller, who was taking a practice Mandatory National Reading and Writing and Math Exam at the public library.

But five seconds into Maude's famous-boycotts-in-history speech, Hillary said, "I don't need a speech, Maude. I won't go to the party. You're right, Miranda *is* rude. I'm surprised I was invited."

Maude shoved a pencil into Hillary's hand.

When Hillary signed, Maude let out a sigh of relief. "Great," she said. "By the way, your answer to question seven is wrong."

After Hillary, Maude went to Donut's house. Donut listened as Maude described famous boy-cotts in history, as well as the story of the hard-boiled egg and the handkerchief. Of all the kids in 3B, Donut understood that Maude was trying to get her classmates to do something impor-tant. But Donut loved doughnuts so much that he couldn't imagine not eating them on purpose.

"I know it's hard, Donut," Maude said. "But we must stand together for Justice!"

Donut, imagining hundreds of doughnuts getting eaten by a white lion, frowned.

"We need to teach the princess a lesson. I was the only kid not invited to the party, remember?"

Donut nodded. He felt bad for Maude. Donut liked Maude, even though he also thought she was very unusual. He felt connected to her, because she knew what it felt like to have a parent who'd died. Donut's father had died, and even though he and Maude never talked about it, Donut felt comforted knowing that there was someone else who felt really sad some days.

His hand was trembling, but he took the pencil from Maude and signed: Duncan David Donatello.

Shocking them both, Maude hugged him.

Then, because she was so happy that she'd gotten every kid in 3B to sign the pledge, which meant she could have her first boycott and first official social justice movement, Maude shared her pack of Rainbow Sweeties with him.

Side by side, they sat on the front porch steps,

looking up at Mount Coffee and eating the stale candy. For a moment, Donut wished he'd gotten to know his dad long enough to find out what his favorite kind of doughnut was. For a moment, Maude wished she could have talked to her mom about having a princess in her class. And then, as their dead parents would have wanted, their minds turned to other things.

# 23

# BIRTHDAY BOYCOTT
# PART ONE

The following Saturday, on the day of the royal birthday party, both Miranda and Maude woke up excited.

Maude whistled as she made her way down to the chicken coop. In just a few hours, Miranda's party would start, and what a shock it would be to that pink princess when no one came. She'd actually done it! The first of many social justice movements!

"Justice for all," Maude sang as she gathered the morning eggs.

"Bawk," Rosalie squawked.

"Good morning, my special Frizzle chicken!" Maude sang. But for some reason her voice sounded weak, not strong. "Your feathers look especially curly this morning."

"Bawk, bawk," Rosalie repeated, looking over

at the other chickens and General Cockatoo, the rooster, who were pecking together in the yard.

Maude looked at the other chickens and then back at Rosalie. "Are you feeling left out of the chicken games?" Maude asked.

Rosalie looked right at her. Could a chicken actually feel left out? *Was it possible that her fancy Frizzle chicken was sad?* Maude wondered. *Of course not*, she told herself, but for some reason she wasn't quite as happy walking up the twenty-seven stairs as she'd been walking down.

On the other side of town, KD and QM led Miranda to an enormous stack of birthday presents.

"Try to open your gifts quickly," KD said. "Since everyone will be coming soon."

Staring at the pile of presents, Miranda shuddered. *Not everyone*, she thought. She hadn't invited Maude. If QM and KD knew Miranda hadn't invited her, they'd probably be mad that she'd broken rule eighty-seven. Maude must have known she'd broken rule eighty-seven, because Maude seemed to know every rule ever invented. She also seemed to know how to finish practice exams quickly and how to avoid playing one of the gross recorders during music class. But still, it was good that Miranda hadn't invited her. Wasn't it?

"Aren't you going to open your present?" QM asked, giving Miranda a puzzled look.

Very slowly, the princess unwrapped the first of many presents before her.

Over at Maude's house, Walt cracked the morning eggs into a sizzling frying pan and said, "The Italian saint Thomas Aquinas once said, 'There is nothing on this earth more to be prized than true friendship.'"

"My chicken Rosalie doesn't seem to have any friends," Maude told him. "I don't know why. She's just like all the other chickens. I mean her feathers are curly since she's a Frizzle, but . . . she's still a chicken, right?"

Michael-John looked up from his dictionary. "A chicken is a chicken is a chicken."

Walt nodded in agreement. "The Irish writer Oscar Wilde once said, 'Be yourself; everyone else is already taken.' Perhaps your curly feathered Rosalie is just being herself."

"Yeah," Maude said. Of course, her chicken couldn't help but be herself. No one could be anything but themselves. Maude couldn't help but be herself. Hillary Greenlight-Miller probably couldn't help but be herself, either. No one could. Not even a princess.

"Eggs, my little stag beetle?" Walt asked.

"No," Maude said. "I'm not hungry."

Back in the castle, KD handed Miranda another gift.

Princess Miranda looked at it glumly.

"Shouldn't you be smiling rainbows?" KD asked. "It's your birthday!"

Miranda shrugged. "I don't feel like opening gifts," she said.

QM, shocked that her daughter didn't want more presents, put her hand on Miranda's forehead.

At the same moment, across town, Walt put his hand on his daughter's forehead, because Maude had never said no to eggs.

"Are you certain you don't want eggs?" Walt asked Maude.

"Go see the white lion," KD suggested. "He's terrifyingly beautiful."

"No, thanks," the princess and the not-a-princess said AT THE EXACT SAME TIME.

It had been a beautiful sunny day, but at that moment, a huge cloud passed over the sun, and everything went dark.

# 24

# BIRTHDAY BOYCOTT
# PART TWO

Although Miranda's party began at noon, she stayed in her pajamas until 11:45 a.m. Then, because it was so late, she put on the first pink dress she saw, which didn't have a single ruffle or sequin. She stared at her shoe collection but decided to go barefoot.

At 11:58 a.m., Miranda walked down the grand staircase, where her parents were waiting. They were shocked by her shoeless feet but said nothing.

At 11:59 a.m., Miranda walked out to the great lawn, where the following happened:

- One dozen pink hot-air balloons rose into the air.
- Thirteen clowns poured out of a tiny automobile.

- The rare white lion roared a terrifying roar.
- Seven screeching monkeys wearing bowties cartwheeled in.
- The castle bells rang out twelve times.

Then everything went silent. Princess Miranda waited.

The clowns stopped laughing, the monkeys stopped screeching, the bells stopped ringing, and the white lion stopped roaring.

Miranda looked all around, and she knew. No one was coming.

# 25

# BIRTHDAY BOYCOTT
# PART THREE

At the very moment Miranda realized no one was coming to her birthday party, Maude glumly put on a plain yellow T-shirt, brown overalls, and sneakers. Slowly, she tied her orange bandana around her neck and walked past Walt, who was standing on his head, and Michael-John, who was reading the definition of the word *onus* (which is a noun meaning burden or blame).

When Maude opened the door, Rudolph Valentino rushed past her and down into the yard. Sluggishly, Maude clomped down the twenty-seven steps after him and knelt beside her huge but tomato-less tomato plant. "Not one tomato? Not one?" Suddenly furious, she began ripping it out of the ground.

When General Cockatoo suddenly crowed, Maude stopped tearing up her plant. She looked

at the dirt in her hands and then over at her rooster, who was hanging with a group of chickens under a shady tree. Then Maude looked at Rosalie in the chicken coop all alone. She imagined Miranda all alone at her party.

Maude wiped the dirt off her hands and rubbed her eyes. Picturing a girl all alone at a party made Maude feel terrible. She knew what that was like. She'd been to parties where everyone else was so busy playing together that they never noticed her swinging alone.

And now Maude had caused that to happen! Her boycott was making someone feel awful! It wasn't social justice at all! Maude pulled her bandana over her eyes, which were tearing. *Ugh,* she thought. Her bandana smelled terrible! She really needed to wash it. No wonder Miranda hadn't wanted to use it on her sneezy nose.

"What have I done?" Maude asked Rudolph Valentino, her stinky bandana, and the broken tomato plant.

Of course, neither the dog nor the bandana nor the plant could answer.

# BIRTHDAY BOYCOTT
## PART FOUR

At 12:05 p.m., Princess Miranda sat down at a party table and put her head on her arms.

At 12:06 p.m., Maude put Rudolph Valentino's leash on and yelled that she was going to take a walk.

"Be home by three!" Walt called.

"I'll try!" Maude yelled back.

"Don't forget what the Greek storyteller Aesop said," Walt called down. "'No act of kindness, no matter how small, is ever wasted.'"

# WHO DOESN'T LOVE CHICKENS?

Without looking at her compass, Maude took eleven lefts and three rights away from her house and, to her surprise, ended up at the very back edge of the castle. She thought about turning around, but instead, she took a step closer. From where she was, she could see ten million pink balloons, a chocolate statue of Miranda, and many adorable monkeys. She took another step and could see the table of doughnuts, a tiny automobile, and a slumped pink figure with bare feet. Maude put on her glasses, took a last step, and stuck her head into an opening in the gate.

At that moment, Miranda looked up and saw Maude. The princess might have been confused by everything in school, but when she saw Maude, she was 100 percent certain that Maude had ruined her party.

When Maude saw Miranda looking at her, she knew that the princess knew that she, Maude, had ruined the party.

Miranda glared at Maude. She hadn't been invited! Why was she here?

But why hadn't Miranda invited her? Because of a dumb drawing in a dumb notebook? *It must have felt awful to be the only one without the gold envelope on her desk*, Miranda thought.

*Miranda must feel terrible to have no one here,* Maude thought. School must be kind of terrible for her, too, since the kids in 3B always stared at her instead of asking her to play on the monkey bars or run around screaming. Maude tried to imagine Miranda running around the playground screaming, but she couldn't. This made Maude a tiny bit happy because she much preferred swinging quietly high above the screaming. Maude wondered what the princess thought about swings.

The two girls looked at one

another for a very long time.

And then Maude yelled, "ARE THOSE RAINBOW SWEETIES?"

*Are those Rainbow Sweeties?* was probably not the best way to end the silent staring. But Maude loved Rainbow Sweeties just as much as Donut loved doughnuts and Miranda loved rearranging all her fancy pink princess things.

Miranda was quiet for so long that Maude thought she hadn't heard her. But then the princess yelled, "YES, THOSE ARE RAINBOW SWEETIES."

At that moment, the white lion roared so ferociously that both girls jumped out of their skin and looked at each other. Then they looked at the white lion, who looked very hungry.

Then something amazing happened. Miranda stood up, went over to the Rainbow Sweeties, scooped some into a bowl, and walked over to Maude.

"Here." Miranda pushed the bowl into Maude's hand. Her *here* was Miranda's way of saying she was sorry that she hadn't invited Maude to the party.

Shocked, Maude pulled her head out of the gate. "Really?"

Miranda nodded.

Maude took the bowl and gulped a handful of candy. Then she remembered the quote Walt had told her about kindness. "Do you want some?" she asked. Maude's *do you want some* was her way of saying she was sorry her boycott had been so successful. And that she'd brought in so many hard-boiled eggs. If she was being honest, she would have admitted that having so many on her desk had been annoying. Maude didn't know that the princess had seen the drawings in her You Journal, but if she did, she would have been sorry about that, too.

Miranda shook her head. "I don't like candy."

Maude was shocked. "Really? What about cake?"

The princess shook her head. "But there's

a very big one if you want some." She pointed toward an enormous pink cake in the middle of the great lawn.

"What about ice cream? Everyone likes ice cream."

"Not me," Miranda said quietly. "I find it too cold. And too sweet."

Maude couldn't believe her ears! Too sweet? "What about doughnuts?" she asked. "Cupcakes? Pudding? Cookies? Pie?" Maude's eyes grew wider as she gobbled another handful of Rainbow Sweeties.

The princess shook her head. "I don't have a sweet tooth."

Maude thought it was incredible that some- one her age didn't like dessert.

Miranda sighed.

"Don't feel bad," Maude said quickly. "Sugar is terrible. I have nine cavities. That's a lot for someone my age. My dad isn't strict about any- thing except for sugar. He hates it! You're more likely to find an antique butterfly sword in my house than one cube of sugar!"

"I don't have any cavities," Miranda said, wondering what an antique butterfly sword was.

"Your teeth are very sparkly and clean."

Miranda nodded, but not rudely.

The girls stared at each other, and then Miranda said, "Wow! You ate that candy fast! Do you want more?" She sounded impressed.

When Maude nodded, the princess pushed a button, the gates opened, and Maude Brandywine Mayhew Kaye entered the castle grounds to follow Princess Miranda across the great lawn.

Then the white lion roared again, which scared the girls so much that their knees and elbows bumped against one another.

"Do you want to get out of here?" Maude asked the princess. "That lion is terrifying. And my dog is really scared." She pointed to Rudolph Valentino, who was shaking and peeing in a far corner of the lawn next to a giant bronze statue of the royal family.

"That's a dog?" Miranda squinted. "I thought it was a rat. A giant rat or a very ugly cat. I hate dogs. I'm terrified of dogs."

Maude smiled kindly at the princess. "Rudolph Valentino is the world's most amazing dog. That's a fact. You're going to love him."

With those five little words, something amazing happened in Miranda's brain. She heard "You're going to love him" as *You're going to love my dog because we're going to be friends and everything is going to get much better.*

"Where do you want to go?" Miranda asked nervously. "Blake, my chauffeur, can only drive me within the town limits."

Maude laughed. "We don't need a ride! We're not climbing Mount Coffee! We'll walk to my house, which is really close. If we go the back way, we're practically neighbors. You can meet my chickens!"

*Walk?* Miranda thought. *You want me to walk somewhere?* She looked down at her feet. It was so weird that she wasn't wearing shoes. "Chickens?" she squeaked out instead.

"Yes! Who doesn't love chickens? I sing to my chickens, so they are the funniest, happiest, most beautiful birds in all the land!"

Miranda continued to stare at her shoeless feet. *Could* she *love chickens?* The princess looked up from her feet and out at the balloons, monkeys, and white lion.

"Plus," Maude said, dumping more Rainbow Sweeties into her pockets and putting her glasses back on, "unlike that terrifying white lion, my chickens won't bite."

The princess looked at Maude, took a deep breath, and said, "Okay. Let's walk to your house."

# 28

# ALL OF THE AMAZING THINGS THAT HAPPENED NEXT

1. Maude went inside the castle while she waited for Miranda to get permission to come over.

2. Miranda asked KD and QM if she could walk to a classmate's house to see some chickens. One of which had curly feathers.

3. "Go," QM said. "Have a wonderful time!"

4. "Don't you want shoes?" KD asked.

5. Miranda ran up to her room, opened her closet, and put on shoes that were almost comfortable!

6. Miranda walked one point two miles! On her own feet!

7. While walking, Miranda thought about calling Blake for a ride 127 times, but she didn't.

8. On a good day, Maude's chickens are

beautiful and hilarious. On this Saturday, they were truly amazing and spectacular.

9. In thirty minutes, both girls were laughing.

10. Most of the girls' laughter was because of the chickens.

11. Some of Maude's laughter was because of all the Rainbow Sweeties she'd eaten.

12. Some of Miranda's laughter was because she'd thrown the world's worst party, was outside the castle by herself, was making a friend, and had walked one point two miles! On her own two feet!

13. Rosalie laid an egg right in front of Miranda.

14. "Weird," Maude said to the princess. "That's her second egg today. It must be a lucky egg. Do you want to get it? Collecting chicken eggs is fun."

15. The princess thought about saying

no way, but instead she walked toward Rosalie and picked up the egg, which was still warm.

16. "Be careful," Maude said. "It's very delicate."

17. "That I know," the princess replied, extremely relieved that just-laid chicken eggs didn't smell nearly as bad as hard-boiled ones.

18. Maude and Miranda carried Rosalie's egg into the house, which meant that Miranda walked up twenty-seven crooked stairs on her own two feet.

19. Michael-John, who was reading dictionaries in his bathrobe, barely looked up when he heard that there was a princess in his house.

20. Walt was not standing on his head.

21. Miranda met Walt, Michael-John, and Onion the Great Number Eleven.

22. Walt, Michael-John, and Onion the Great Number Eleven met Miranda.

23. Walt took Rosalie's egg and some other eggs and made a delicious omelet for

Maude and Miranda, who realized they were both starving.

24. Miranda was making a friend.

25. Maude was making a friend.

26. In just six hours, the princess and the absolutely not a princess discovered that they had lots to talk about, including: the wonderfulness of Miss Kinde, the awfulness of Hillary Greenlight-Miller, the loudness

of Principal Fish, the grossness of school lunches, the yuckiness of the practice Mandatory National Reading and Writing and Math Exam, and the greatness of cheese.

27. It turned out that Maude and Miranda both really loved cheese!

28. When it was time for Miranda to go home, she was shocked to see it was nearly dark. She'd never spent so long laughing with someone her age.

29. Walt gave the girls headlamps, and they walked the one point two miles back, which meant that in one day, Miranda had walked two point four miles! On her very own feet!

30. Maude would have walked back to her house, but because it was dark, QM and KD insisted that Blake drive her, so Maude got to ride in the fancy automobile!

# 29

# FANTASTIC THINGS AND INCREDIBLE IDEAS

After all the amazing things that happened after the birthday boycott, the princess and the absolutely not a princess were friends. Friends! Maude Brandywine Mayhew Kaye and Princess Miranda Rose Lapointsetta talked and whispered and giggled with each other so much that Miss Kinde often thought about separating them. She didn't, though. Partly because she liked alphabetical order, but mostly because she was so pleased to see two girls who had seemed so different discover they had so much in common.

With the exception of Hillary Greenlight-Miller, 3B was happy that Maude and the princess were friends. Hillary was jealous that she didn't have a princess for a best friend, and she devoted even more time to her Saturday practice Mandatory National Reading and Writing

and Math Exams. For about a week, Donut was irritated that the table of birthday doughnuts had been devoured by the insatiable white lion instead of him, but eventually he got over it.

Amazing things started happening for Miranda now that she had a friend. Because she walked over to Maude's house a lot, she was finally getting enough exercise and went right to sleep on school nights, which meant she wasn't so tired at school. Not being so tired meant she understood more, too. She still needed extra-extra help, but Maude was almost as good at explaining things as Miss Kinde.

Maude discovered that it was fun to help a best friend learn new things. And some days Maude learned from Miranda! She didn't learn new vocabulary words or how to grow tomatoes, but she learned that if she laid out her clothes the night before like the princess did, then she could almost make it to school on time. Maude also learned that hanging out with a friend in a castle was even better than she could have imagined.

Castles, it turned out, were not only full of rare books, uncomfortable furniture, and very large paintings. They were also full of candy, water-beds, and really big televisions! Even though Maude was into justice for all, growing tomatoes, and taking long walks, she also really loved tele-vision. Walt felt the same way about television as he did about sugar, so Maude didn't have a tele-vision at her house.

One recent Saturday morning, Maude roller-skated over to the castle with Rudolph Valentino.

"Hello!" she called to QM and KD, who, as usual, were sitting on their uncomfortable couch in their uncomfortable clothes in one of the castle's beautiful sitting rooms.

"Good morn—" QM and KD called as Maude flew past them and up to Miranda's wing.

"I'm starving!" Maude announced to the princess, who was organizing her nail polishes. "I'm just going to call the kitchen and order a little something." She pushed the castle intercom button down to the kitchen.

The princess smiled to herself, since Maude had said the same exact thing last Saturday and the Saturday before that.

By the time Chef Blue knocked on the princess's door to deliver Maude's banana split with extra hot fudge on the side, bowl of Rainbow Sweeties, and French fries, Maude was completely zoned out in front of the enormous television. Miranda put down the bottle of "plumtastic plum" and walked across the room to get Maude's food.

"Thank you," Miranda said to Chef Blue.

"You're most welcome," Chef Blue replied, grinning at Maude, who was grinning at the TV. Even if it was much too early for dessert, Chef Blue loved being able to finally make sweets for a child.

Miranda brought Maude her food and went back to her polishes. But after she finished putting "lovely lemon" next to "midnight madness" she decided she was bored.

"Let's do something," Miranda said.

Maude nodded at the TV.

"Maude," Miranda said a little louder.

"How adorable," Maude cooed to the pair of juggling cats.

Miranda walked in front of the TV and started doing jumping jacks.

"You're blocking the enormous television," Maude whined.

"Let's *do* something," Miranda said. "I don't want to watch TV all day."

"You don't?" Maude asked.

"No." Miranda said. "Let's go to your house. Did you collect eggs? I miss the chickens."

"The chickens are molting," Maude said.

"Molting means losing or shedding feathers," the princess replied.

"Good practice Mandatory National Reading and Writing and Math Exam word!" Maude looked away from the TV and smiled at her friend. "But when chickens molt they stop laying eggs." She dipped a French fry in hot fudge and looked back at the TV. "Let's hang out here till lunch."

The princess felt disappointed. Lunch wasn't for several hours, and now that she went to school, she'd gotten used to spending time out of the castle. The things at Maude's house weren't fancy, but they were always fascinating. Not only was there Walt's enormous beetle collection, there were also things like pirate swords and false-teeth bottle openers just lying around. At the castle, most of the really interesting things were locked away.

"I want to do something now," Miranda said.

"Like what?"

Miranda looked around. She noted the neatly arranged fashion magazines on her desk, the fabric samples near her closet, and Rudolph Valentino curled up on her bed. She walked over and gave him a pet, then looked at Maude, who was wearing orange overalls and a brand-new, almost-clean purple bandana. Maude had kicked off her shoes and roller skates. Her socks, Miranda noticed, were an odd shade of green and full of holes. Then Miranda looked at her almost perfectly alphabetized nail-polish collection.

"I have an idea!" She smiled.

"What?" Maude asked, suddenly nervous.

"Let's paint your toenails."

Maude put on her glasses and stared at Miranda.

"I'll take it off if you don't like it," Miranda said. "Promise."

"I won't like it," Maude said. She pushed her glasses up to the top of her head. "I refuse pink."

Miranda scanned her polishes until she landed on "transcendent turquoise." She held it up. "How's this?"

Maude sighed. "Don't tell anyone. Whoever heard of a social justice activist with fancy feet?"

"I won't."

"And," Maude said, "if I let you polish my toes, you're going to have to do something, too."

"Like what?"

"I'll think of something." Maude smiled mischievously. "But don't worry, I won't make you eat a hard-boiled egg." Now that Maude knew how much Miranda hated hard-boiled eggs, she only ate them when the princess wasn't around.

Miranda began painting her best friend's toes. A long time passed, and then she stepped away. "It's amazing," the princess said. Maude's feet did look incredible.

"I can't look," Maude said, covering her eyes.

"Really?" Miranda was disappointed, but not surprised.

"Sorry," Maude said. "I'm ready to walk back to my house now so you can have your turn." She swallowed the last French fry and tried to give Miranda her most sinister smile.

Truthfully, Maude was having a hard time deciding what she could have Miranda do in exchange for the nail polish on her toes. She tried to come up with a brilliant idea while the two girls walked back to her house, checked on the still-molting chickens, and climbed up the slightly crooked twenty-seven stairs into her house. Unfortunately, the princess had already organized all Maude's overdue library books (by color) and straightened all of the protest posters on her walls. She could have Miranda rearrange her closet, which was about to explode, but that would be too much fun for the princess. Maude looked around her room, hoping for an idea as bananas as nail polish.

Her eyes landed on the big pile of dirty clothes on her floor. *Eureka*, she thought, scooping up an armful and walking over to her friend, who was singing to Rudolph Valentino.

"Here ya go," Maude said, holding out a bright orange T-shirt and a pair of cargo pants with holes in the knees.

The princess looked up from the dog. "These are your clothes," she said.

Maude grinned.

"What . . . do you want me to do with them?" *Organize them*, the princess hoped Maude would say. She'd like nothing more than to tidy Maude's very messy room.

"Wear them." Maude smiled. "It's your part of the deal." She waved her foot in front of the princess. The shiny blue polish gleamed in the sunlight streaming through Maude's window.

Maude's toenails did look terrific, but the princess felt ill. Even though having a best friend had made her much happier, she was still picky about clothes. But she knew that a deal was a deal, so she slowly took off her fancy shoes, silk pants, and very expensive shirt. Reminding herself how much better school was with a friend, she slid into Maude's filthy pants. Next, she put on the stained orange shirt that read I'M + I LOST AN ELECTRON, a joke that she didn't get because she was still behind in science.

When she looked in Maude's mirror, Miranda did a double take. Everything was small, smelled like chicken feathers, and felt strangely warm. On the other hand, nothing poked or itched. Maude's dirty clothes felt soft and broken in.

Miranda hadn't felt this comfortable ever.

Maude picked up one of Miranda's golden shoes. "This is really heavy," she said. "How do you wear it?"

"On my foot," the princess said.

Maude put the shoe on. Then she put on the other one and attempted to stand up.

Miranda tried to hide her giggle as she looked at Maude wearing the gold shoes.

Maude looked at Miranda in the I'M + I LOST AN

ELECTRON shirt and turned
her laugh into a cough.

Michael-John knocked
on the door. "Dad wants to
know if the princess and
the absolutely not a prin-
cess want vittles," he said. "*Vittles*
is a plural noun that means food.
Right now, it's lunch."

"What's for lunch?" Miranda
asked through the closed door.

"Stinky bishop cheese, bread,
and tomatoes—not from Maude's garden,"
Michael-John replied.

*Stinky bishop cheese*, the princess thought,
rubbing Maude's shirt. That sounded like it would
smell. Not that long ago, she never would've let
anyone see her in Maude's clothes. But having had
twenty-seven days of best friendship, she knew
that if life were to be an amazing adventure, you
had to try a new cheese every now and then.

"Don't laugh," Maude told her brother as she
opened the door.

As soon as Michael-John saw Maude and Miranda, he howled with laughter. When he finally stopped laughing, he took Maude's glasses from the top of her head and handed them to the princess.

"Do I have to?" Miranda asked.

"Yes," Michael-John said. "Maude isn't Maude without her glasses."

Miranda sighed and put the glasses on.

And then, in a flash, the world to Princess Miranda was CLEAR!

For the first time, the princess noticed the scar on Michael-John's chin, the blueness of Maude's eyes, how lovely Rudolph Valentino's fur really was.

"Miranda?" Maude and Michael-John asked together, staring at the princess.

But Miranda couldn't speak. Her eyes grew wide as she walked around the house, noticing the masks on the walls, the plants in the living room, the containers of preserved beetles, and the pile of dictionaries on the dining room table. In a daze, she couldn't stop marveling at the clear and colorful world she lived in.

"Miranda?" Maude asked her friend with great concern. "Are you okay?"

Miranda looked up to Maude and Michael-John's curious faces. "I can see!" she exclaimed. "And my headache is gone!"

# 30

# WHERE THE STORY ENDS

Sadly, this is the end. Except in many ways, just like the friendship between absolutely not a princess Maude Brandywine Mayhew Kaye and Princess Miranda Rose Lapointsetta, it's just the beginning. There's much more ahead!

On this lovely autumn afternoon, the two friends are laughing as they walk on their own two feet. There they go, arm in arm, one in fancy shoes, the other smelling like chickens, headed in the direction of clear sight, school, friendship, and even more amazing adventures.

# ACKNOWLEDGMENTS

This book is for my daughters, Georgia and Dahlia. Without the two of you, the two girls in this book wouldn't exist.

# EMMA WUNSCH

Emma Wunsch is the author of *The Movie Version*, a young adult novel. This is her first chapter book. She lives in Lebanon, New Hampshire, with her husband and two daughters.

**VISIT HER ONLINE AT
EMMAWUNSCH.COM
AND MIRANDAANDMAUDE.COM**

# JESSIKA VON INNEREBNER

Jessika von Innerebner is an artist
who's worked with clients including Disney,
Nickelodeon, Highlights, and Fisher-Price.
She lives in Kelowna, Canada.

**VISIT HER ONLINE AT
JESSVONI.COM**